PSYCHOSIA
THE UNEXPLAINED DISORDER

PSYCHOSIA
THE UNEXPLAINED DISORDER

PSYCHOSIA
THE UNEXPLAINED DISORDER

Psychosia
The Unexplained Disorder

PSYCHOSIA
THE UNEXPLAINED DISORDER

PSYCHOSIA
THE UNEXPLAINED DISORDER

Psychosia
The Unexplained Disorder

~ Lena Ma

PSYCHOSIA
THE UNEXPLAINED DISORDER

PSYCHOSIA
THE UNEXPLAINED DISORDER

TABLE OF CONTENTS

PSYCHOSIA
THE UNEXPLAINED DISORDER

PSYCHOSIA
THE UNEXPLAINED DISORDER

PSYCHOSIA
THE UNEXPLAINED DISORDER

CHAPTER ONE

Hospitalized

"Son of a bitch! Get off! Get off! Stop touching me! I am a strong and independent woman! I deserve to be free! I do not deserve this endless torture. I deserve mercy! I deserve love! I deserve attention! Let me go! Let me go! Free me!!"

A pleading and despairing scream pierces the stark silence from a distance. It reverberates through the echoing halls and shatters the barred windows of a well-renowned psychiatric hospital.

Staff who pride themselves on inflicting excruciating torture and torment on their patients refuse to flinch as they blankly stare at patient zero, emotionless and detached.

"Let go of me! You can't detain me! I have rights! I refuse to be your prisoner!"

Blair Pevensie's grating voice resonates loudly throughout the quarantined and sequestered hospital, where she stands surrounded by seven medical professionals and patients.

The hospital lies deep inside obscure and overgrown woods, surrounded by electrical barbed wires and shallow tunnels. No one in. No one out. More importantly, no one could hear when the patients cried.

"You can't control me! You have no right to touch me! I deserve to live!" Blair's voice continues to crash down the halls.

Nonetheless, no one is touching her. No one is restraining her. No one is even near her, a reality that Blair is unable to comprehend as she swears to herself that she is being tackled to the floor by a group of stout medical professionals.

Blair is delusional. Her thoughts are no longer lucid. She can no longer see who she is, much less who she was. All she can perceive are the demons that surround her, forcing her to lash out at and segregate herself from others.

However, Blair does not hallucinate. She does not see people who do not exist nor does she hear voices that are not speaking to her. Instead, she feels controlled by certain powerful forces that cause her to behave in ways she cannot understand or remember.

Her mind feels out of place, wandering like it doesn't belong to her body.

She cannot help but feel vehement and sadistic during her most apprehensive moments, with her thoughts pushing her to engage in conflicting and contradictory deeds.

Sometimes, her thoughts become so penetrating that her mind feels ready to detonate, and she imposes agony onto herself in attempts to subdue her pulsating insanity.

***

Suddenly, Blair feels overpowered with ire. She hastily glances around her surroundings and spots a glass vase filled with beautiful roses, sitting on the nurses' station. She bolts over to the station, pushing an ancient-looking nurse onto the ground for standing in her way.

The nurse falls onto the cement ground of the ward's lobby; the side of her skull fractures as she bleeds out onto the floor. The other nurses on call scream in horror as a swarm of security guards rush toward Blair.

Before Blair can be restrained, she grabs the vase and, without thinking, heaves it at a patient who sits calmly on a rusty chair. Fortunately, the vase misses the man's head by a hair and smashes against the brick wall.

The man freezes for a second and then begins to chuckle. He suffers from psychosis and finds acts of violence humorous. However, the other patients do not remain as carefree and nonchalant as he does.

They panic, creating a stampede as they push and trample over those in their way. Fearful, the nurses quickly round up the patients and confine them behind the nurses' station, protected and sheltered from Blair's circadian outbreaks.

"Fuck you! Don't fucking touch me!" Blair bellows, swinging her arms maniacally as two heavily-armed security guards wrestle her onto the ground.

Swinging her slender legs, Blair kicks one of the guards across his face and forcefully bites into the arm of the other. She barely makes a dent, only a tiny scratch, on the two brawny men.

The guards finally pin her to the ground, the patients cheering as they see their worst nightmare go down...once again.

"Wilson, grab the straitjacket. This is going to be a long night," Emily, the nurse supervisor, commands her intern.

On her orders, Wilson runs down the vacant halls and retrieves a straitjacket from the locked supply closet, the same one that Blair had worn just yesterday. With the help of the guards, the nurses struggle to strap Blair in.

However, Blair does not make it easy, continuing to kick and bite the nurses as they fight to snap her into the jacket. Blair screams as she experiences immense pain and betrayal, her wrath eventually subsiding as she becomes breathless and weak.

***

"Psychotic and Demented. Keep in Solitary Confinement."

That is what the door to Blair's cell says, the steel and gated door chained with locks and bolts that does not provide an easy access through to either side.

The guards thrust Blair into her cell and shackle her to the wall. She didn't use to be cuffed. Hell, she used to sleep in a normal room like the rest of the patients, with a soft bed, a functioning toilet, and an unlocked door she could freely walk in and out of.

When Blair was first admitted to Eloquoia Psychiatric Hospital, she seemed as normal as any other. She spent her first few weeks in silence, mindlessly swallowing unknown pills and speaking minimal words during therapy sessions. She nibbled on her tasteless meals and scuttled into bed in the early evenings to watch her days of hell pass by faster.

But then something changed. A click. A switch. A demonic voice that had set an overcast of hate and insanity above her head. She began to flicker with conflicting emotions, loving life one moment and cutting into herself the next.

Her most unforgettable moment was during CBT group therapy last summer. Blair had just finished unleashing her thoughts and feelings of her lost love and accepted the consoling words of others in the group.

However, soon after another patient began sharing memories about her own relationship, Blair shrieked and started clawing into herself with her fingernails. She was immediately taken to the emergency room as blood covered her entire body, alarming the other patients.

Now Blair has restricted contact with anyone outside her own chamber. She needs to be constantly monitored during group therapies, and she eats her meals in the corner of her locked cell, next to the bucket she uses to relieve herself. She tried to drown herself in the toilet once, just once, and look where that got her.

Blair is chained like a prisoner, with no end or hope of escape in sight. She has completely lost her freedom; every moment is constantly being watched. She has not bathed or showered in months as she is only allowed to be washed by a nurse.

Unfortunately, many of the nurses refuse to go near her for fear of their own safety.

Kiersten Addison, the only nurse with enough courage to step foot near Blair, walks behind the station, crushes half a bottle of sedatives, and sprinkles them into a glass of water.

Having been a nurse for over 20 years, Kiersten is used to patients behaving erratically, and Blair is no exception. Blair had lunged at Kiersten more than a few times. She wanted to exert supremacy over all the nurses by instilling trepidation into them.

Unfortunately for her, Kiersten feels no fear. After she was stabbed in the chest, thankfully missing her heart, by another patient who experienced a psychotic breakdown 10 years ago, she had trained herself to stare death in the face and not be rattled. Sure, Blair had bitten her several times, but nothing she could not handle.

Kiersten takes out her key and unlocks one of the bolts barricading the door to Blair's dungeon. She proceeds to unchain the rest of the locks and lets herself into Blair's quarters. Blair had been deemed so dangerous that she is now sealed in a box that takes over 20 minutes to unlock.

"Help me."

Kiersten hears a faint whisper in the background as she deadbolts the door behind her to ensure that Blair would not push her over and try to escape. Kiersten turns around and sees Blair hanging in her usual spot, her head facing the ground, with tears dripping from her face.

She walks toward Blair, stopping less than an inch from her face.

"Help me," Blair whispers again, her body twitching intermittently.

Kiersten reaches her hand up to Blair's face, but before she could soothe her, Blair turns demonic once again.

"Get the fuck out of my room! I hate you! I hate everyone! Stop hurting me! Get out! Get out! Get out! Get away from me! You can't have me!"

Kiersten swiftly jerks her hand away just before Blair can bite her. She has been with Blair since she was first admitted to Eloquoia.

Back then, Blair was an introverted and compassionate young woman, always behaving and never seeming like she would hurt a soul. Now she has become someone, or rather something, that Kiersten no longer recognizes.

When Blair is not erratic, she looks like a helpless little girl, fearful of death and disappointment. She used to be an obedient person, catering to and pleasing the needs of others before her own. What changed?

Kiersten treads toward Blair again and lifts the glass of water up to Blair's lips. Blair refuses, and instead, spits in Kiersten's face. Luckily for Kiersten, Blair had done this before.

She pulls out what she likes to call "The Pryr," a device that allows medical professionals to pry open the mouths of ferocious or involuntary patients from afar.

Kiersten pries open Blair's mouth, attaching her end of the device to the metal bars of the door. She walks toward Blair, roughly lifts her head by pushing against her chin, and pours the water down her throat. This forces Blair to either swallow or choke, allowing Kiersten to shove nearly half the glass into her.

Kiersten then disconnects the device, steps back, and moments later, Blair slowly drifts asleep.

'She's getting worse by the minute,' Kiersten contemplates to herself as she exits Blair's dungeon. 'Every day is the same. Anger. Rage. Lockdown. Anger. Rage. Lockdown. At this rate, she's never going to get out of here. She's never going to get better. She's only in her twenties. She has her entire life ahead of her, yet she spends most of her days inside a cell, jumping from hospital to hospital. I tried with her. I really wanted her to get better. I had such high hopes. I gave her everything she needed to recover. Now I feel ready to give up on her. She just doesn't seem to be trying anymore.'

***

"Kiersten?" Blair slurs docilely after what felt like a minute of sleep.

She opens her eyes and sees that she is still chained to the wall.

"What happened?" Blair questions to herself.

The last event she recollects was her revolting outbreak in the hospital lobby.

"I must have blacked out."

Blair cannot remember much these days. Her memories seem to flash in and out, and she can only recall few sporadic moments. She had been chained to the wall before, many times. However, she never seems to remember as anxiety overwhelms her each time.

Blair tries to call out to Nurse Kiersten, but her throat begins to close, preventing her from being able to speak, almost as if her voice had suddenly vanished. She tries to open her mouth again. Nothing.

'Fucking hell!' Blair tries to scream as she quickly realizes that her voice remains in her own head.

Suddenly, out of nowhere, Blair feels a burning sensation on the skin of her stomach that gets worse with each breath she takes. Her skin feels like it is on fire as her stomach is being torn apart from the inside out, with a sharp knife carving deep into her muscles.

Petrified and feeling immense brutality, Blair pulls out the metal wire she stashes in between her brunette locks and picks open the cuffs that restrain her. She then fumbles to rip through the straitjacket that immobilized her arms, biting and shredding pieces of fabric off until she finally scratches through and falls onto the ground. She pulls the jacket over her head, lifts her gown, and examines her abdomen.

To her disbelief and bewilderment, Blair does not see anything. Her skin is not peeling off, and her stomach is not on fire. No one is slicing her with a knife nor is her gown piercing her. Then why is she experiencing this sweltering sensation?

Then she feels something. Bumps. Scars. She can smell an aroma of her own blood. She brings her hands up to her face and sees her fingers covered in blood. She looks down and sees bloody red cuts on the left side of her abdomen.

'What? What the hell is this?!' Blair wonders as her breath staggers and mind spins.

There is no one else in sight, but disturbingly, more and more cuts are appearing on her body, almost as if an invisible spirit is slashing her.

Blair screeches, finding her voice once again. The pain intensifies to the point where her body is in so much anguish that she feels anesthetized. She cries out again, but no one comes to her rescue.

Blair's psychosis causes her to react so melodramatically that it becomes difficult for anyone to believe whether she is actually in pain or whether she is only acting out.

"Why won't anyone help me? Help me! Make it stop! Leave me alone! Help!"

Blair continues to scream as pools of tears rain from her eyes, dripping onto the cold and damp ground. She has experienced so many psychotic breaks that it becomes challenging for even her to distinguish what is reality.

During these moments, she feels imprisoned inside her own body, unable to escape. She feels as if someone else is controlling her, and she cannot remove herself from the grasps of this mysterious person.

Abruptly, Blair stops screaming as sees words beginning to form, words hidden among the many incisions already on her body.

"El...el...peh...elp....elpee...heh...," Blair reads as she struggles to make out what the words say.

The carving stops, and Blair leans her head over to read.

"HELP ME."

"Help me?" Blair reiterates. "What the hell does that mean? Help who?"

Unbeknownst, memories and flashbacks of past harrowing moments flash before her eyes. Then she remembers. "Help me." These two words might as well make up her entire vocabulary.

Over the past decade, she has written and screamed these words wherever and whenever she could, sometimes out of necessity, but mostly due to her cravings for attention.

Maybe karma really is a bitch. Maybe after all these years, the two words that she had come to call her "friends" have now come back as her "enemies" to haunt her. Maybe this is how her life ends, carved into like a turkey until she finally bleeds out and dies.

'What am I even running from anymore? Why should I still care if I live? None of it matters. I don't know what life feels like outside of bars. Maybe I should just give up. Maybe I should just relinquish and perish,' Blair ruminates to herself.

Kiersten calmly enters the chamber just as Blair coughs up blood, lying ill and helpless on the ground. Blood drips from her eyes as she looks up and sees the emotionless face of Nurse Kiersten.

"Nurse...help me. Please help me," Blair cries out feebly, unsure of whether to feel defeated or powerful.

"Blair...what are you doing?"

"I said fucking help me! Help me!" Blair cries out again, this time with more rage and demand.

"Blair...stop."

"Get it off! Get it off! Get it off me!" Blair continues to shriek.

Kiersten watches, her mind wandering as Blair repeatedly scratches her stomach and arms. Three times a week, Blair's cell is cleansed and sanitized because of her self-inflicted injuries during her outbreaks. She claims she cannot control her psychotic breaks and swears she cannot remember these events the following day.

However, Blair had fucked with the minds of everyone too much during her stay. Nobody believes a word she says anymore.

"Blair, stop. There's nothing on you," Kiersten speaks, her voice low.

"Get it off me! It's hurting me! Make it stop! Please!"

"Blair!" Kiersten screams, finally fed up, as she slaps Blair across the face. "There's nothing on you! You're imagining it again!"

With the sound of Kiersten's voice, Blair snaps back into reality, unable to recall what had just happened.

"Blair, what the hell was that?" Kiersten solicits.

"What the hell was what?" Blair retorts innocently.

"You were literally just screaming in pain about something persecuting you. Do you not remember?"

"What are you talking about? I've been asleep for the past hour and woke up to you slamming on my door. I think you're the crazy one here, not me," Blair jokes as an attempt to use humor to distract from discomfort.

"Alright, Blair. You need to cut the crap right now! I'm tired of your lies, and I'm tired of your drama. You need to be straight with me right now! Do you remember what you just did?" Kiersten demands as she squeezes Blair's arms.

"Ouch! Stop! You're hurting me!" Blair shouts. "Let go, or I'm calling the cops on you!"

Kiersten is only thirty-five, but over a decade of dealing with psychotic patients has taken a toll on her, making her appear as if she's in her sixties. Defeated, Kiersten gently picks Blair up off the ground.

"Come on, let's get you cleaned up," Kiersten quietly whispers.

"I'm not crazy...," Blair murmurs behind Kiersten as she leads her toward the bathroom.

"I know. I know. But I am going to need you to hand over that wire."

"I don't have it."

"What do you mean 'you don't have it'? Where is it?" Kiersten questions exasperatingly.

"It's...it's...inside me."

Kiersten is not surprised. Blair has done this before, shoving wires and nails inside her body to avoid having them taken away from her. Blair always has the intention of relieving herself later to retrieve the items, but time after time, she fails to do so, unable to learn from her past mistakes.

'Son of an ass. I hate prying shit out of there,' Kiersten thinks to herself, fed up with Blair's impulsive and disgusting actions.

With her arm around her nurse, Blair slowly walks toward the lavatory. Blair never goes into the bathroom alone. She lost that privilege when she was found bleeding out in the tub after cutting herself with a piece of plastic from the smashed toilet cover.

After that incident, the hospital signed a decree that a nurse must be by Blair's side whenever she needs to go in. However, the nurses at Eloquoia often refuse to volunteer for that task as they had all been bitten by Blair whenever they touched her.

Because of this, Blair spends more time than not relieving herself in a stench-filled bucket and going weeks at a time without bathing or showering.

"Alright, bend over," Nurse Kiersten instructs Blair as she locks both her and herself inside the lavatory.

"Fuck you," Blair stutters.

"What did you say to me?" Kiersten asks, fully aware.

"I said, fuck you! I am not fucking bending over, and there's nothing you can do about it, you bitch!" Blair screams.

Blair keeps changing, as if she has multiple personalities. No one could ever figure out her condition. She exhibits all the behaviors of every mental illness in the book, yet possesses none of the symptoms to be classified as one.

That is why it has been so difficult to treat her. Blair has become a lost cause in the eyes of every doctor and nurse across the country. No one believes she can be saved. No one wants to continue trying. Everyone, including her own family, has given up on her.

"Alright, alright. Fine. Let's get you cleaned up then. Is that okay with you? You smell like you haven't showered in months."

Unenthusiastically, Blair agrees, completely switching personalities once again.

Kiersten tenderly removes the gown from Blair's body, careful to not tear her skin as parts of the gown had submerged into her deep self-inflicted wounds. Blair is no longer timid about being naked in front of the nurse. Her humility and shame had vanished long before she was admitted into Eloquoia. Besides, it was nothing Kiersten had not seen by this point.

Kiersten fills the small tub with icy water. The government had cut funding for Eloquoia decades ago due to their unconventional and inhumane treatment methods. In fact, they were shut down twelve years ago when piles of patients' bodies had been discovered, buried under burnt rags and ashes, beneath the nearby campground.

Blair yelps as Kiersten picks her up and drops her into the freezing water. She thrashes her arms wildly and kicks the sides of the tub, splitting the shower curtain as Kiersten tries to prevent her from biting into her shoulder.

Minutes later, Blair passes out from the chilling shock as Kiersten soothingly washes her.

***

Life has not always been this way for Blair. She didn't use to be this crazy lunatic who cannot be trusted to speak or act with integrity. She didn't use to spend her days chained up and branded as "the maniacal outcast." She used to be, well, normal.

Every time Blair attempts to remember her life before this living hell, her mind always flashes back to the events that caused her life to spiral downhill forever.

Unfortunately, she cannot recall the exact moments that caused her downward spiral. Hell, for all she knows, it could have very well been caused by monotony and lonesomeness.

She reminiscences the night where she had locked herself inside her bedroom out of resentment and frustration from her multiple failed attempts at online dating. She does not handle rejection well. Rejection makes her entire body cringe as the feeling drives her to tear into her own skin and rip out her beating black heart.

After a man, a man whom she didn't even find attractive, called her an "ugly freak" and blocked her, she walked into her bathroom and insulted herself in her mirror before smashing the glass with her fist. She then rummaged through her drawers and pulled out a razor blade.

Taking a pair of old scissors, she cut down the middle of her black corset, exposing her bare midriff, and began carving the words "HELP ME" with the blade on her stomach while laughing maniacally to herself.

With each cut, crimson blood dripped from her inflicted wounds onto the white-tiled floor of the bathroom. Each slice created more and more blood loss and lightheadedness. She carved one last cut, underlining the words before collapsing onto the floor, blood pooling out of her lifeless body as she prayed for death.

Perhaps she would have gotten her wish had her parents not found her two seconds too soon. After noticing that the faucet had been left running, with no reply from Blair after screaming up at her to stop wasting water, they went upstairs. Her father was ready to kick open the door and reprimand his daughter until he saw a pool of blood seep out from underneath the bathroom door.

Panicking, her father raced downstairs to grab a crowbar. When he returned, he pried open the door to find Blair cataleptic and hemorrhaging as her mother darted to call an ambulance.

As the paramedics tried to resuscitate her, Blair's mother cried. She sat beside her daughter inside the ambulance, holding onto her hand as her father paced back and forth, cursing to himself. Blair had pulled this before for attention, and he cannot believe he had let it happen again. The ambulance detoured through several unfamiliar streets and two obscure forests before finally reaching the old barred building of Eloquoia, the country's oldest psychiatric facility.

***

Blair's memories then flash to a picture of a gentleman, a handsome gentleman with chestnut brown hair, piercing blue eyes, and a chiseled jawline featuring a warm yet sensual smile. He holds a bouquet of flowers and reaches his other hand out toward Blair.

"Aiden," Blair whispers, awakening as she nearly drowns in the tub after her head slips off the edge.

"Blair, what the hell is wrong with you!? Are you alright?" Nurse Kiersten exclaims.

"What happened?" Blair asks, confused.

"You were crying," Kiersten responds.

'Crying?' Blair brings her left hand up to her face.

Her cheeks feel damp, but she does not sense sadness or pain. She often cannot remember shedding tears until after she has done so. Have her emotions become so detached from her conscious mind that she no longer experiences feelings?

"I'm alright," Blair responds, brushing the tears away from her face.

Not convinced, Kiersten helps Blair out of the bath and hands her a towel to dry herself off before changing into a new hospital gown, turquoise this time. Blair can never wear the same color two days in a row.

Eloquoia specially orders multicolor gowns just for her. The last time they tried to force her to wear a white gown two days in a row, Blair nearly killed a patient. She bit into him and held him hostage until they gave her a different one.

"What do you want to do today?" Kiersten asks.

"I'm hungry. Can I go to lunch?" Blair pleads.

"Okay, you wait right here. I'll go get your tray for you."

"No, not here. I want to go to the cafeteria."

Blair is usually prohibited from eating lunch with the other patients. Her volatile temper tantrums and viciousness toward the other patients mandated her to eat in seclusion in her own prison. Many of the suicidal patients at Eloquoia find her triggering, only making it worse when Blair tells them to "just get over it."

"Fine, I suppose we can go today. But you need to promise me that you'll behave. One word or riot out of you, and we're out. Do you understand?" Kiersten demands.

Blair half-heartedly nods, and Kiersten escorts her to the cafeteria after locking the bathroom door.

Upon stepping foot into the cafeteria, close quarters barely enough to fit two tables and ten patients, Blair begins to feel immense remorse and sorrow for herself.

'How did I end up here, in this locked compartment with all these sick and old people? I'm not sick. There's nothing wrong with me. What the hell did I do to myself? Maybe I shouldn't have lied. Maybe I shouldn't have harmed myself for attention. But I had to. No one would care about me otherwise. No one was paying attention to me. I was beginning to feel forgotten and ignored. What else was I supposed to do? I needed to feel loved. I still need to feel loved. Acting out is the only way I can get people to notice me. There's never any other way. Is there? Is this who I've become? Is this who I am now? Is it too late to turn back? Is all hope lost for me?'

With this thought, Blair freezes in place as she stares at some patients monotonously pace back and forth while others consume their food one grain at a time.

The cafeteria is the only room in the entire building where patients can have visitors. Blair continues to stare as she sees a few patients talking and laughing with their families. She becomes envious as parents hug and kiss their children, telling them that they are not alone and will get through these difficult times.

A feeling of nostalgia suddenly rushes through her. Blair misses her family, her parents, and her friends. If only she had appreciated them more rather than scaring them away when they came to visit, maybe she wouldn't be so lonely right now. But now it's too late. They're all gone. During their last visit, she told them to drop dead and never return. Now she wishes she could take back her words as isolation begins to set in hard.

When Blair was first admitted to Eloquoia, her family visited her every day. They brought her clean clothes, and they talked and laughed with her, just like the other families. However, after one of Blair's therapy sessions triggered her paranoia, she bit off her father's ear after thinking that her family was scheming to keep her trapped in the psych ward forever.

Since then, they have not stepped foot back into the hospital. They fear the day they must come face to face with Blair again. Her memory of that moment haunts her to this day as trauma begins to devastate her.

"Okay, we're here. Do you want your lunch?" Kiersten asks, breaking the tension.

"No," Blair responds, her voice hostile and cold.

"No?" An annoyance shines through Kiersten's voice.

"I'm not hungry anymore. I need to get out of here. Take me back."

"But I thought you said you're hungry."

"Take me back!" Blair shrieks as she picks up a metal chair and hurls it at the boarded-up windows.

PSYCHOSIA
THE UNEXPLAINED DISORDER

CHAPTER TWO

Scorned

"Blair, it's time to get up," Kiersten declares as she nudges Blair to wake up for her daily medications.

It is four in the morning, and every morning is the same. Kiersten shines a bright light in Blair's eyes to wake up the beast. She then gives her medications that Blair just conceals under her tongue and spits out when Kiersten isn't looking.

Blair's eyes flutter open as she remains chained to her metal bedframe. The thin mattress barely provides enough padding for comfort. Under hospital law, Blair must either remain chained or handcuffed even when she is in her own quarters.

The psychiatrists say it's to prevent her from potentially hurting herself. However, Blair is certain there is something far more sinister behind her entrapment. Her freedom and independence were taken away from her when she was deemed psychologically unfit to be around herself or others without imposing maltreatment. The only times she can regain a sense of liberty outside of chains are when Kiersten supervises her.

"Are you ready for your appointment today with Dr. Gwenneth?" Kiersten optimistically asks as she gently brushes Blair's hair.

"Do I really have to go? I hate that woman," Blair whines.

Marleigh Gwenneth is a stern psychiatrist dedicated to intimidating patients, and it's easy to see why. The woman never smiles, her eyes always slightly narrow, and her nose creases to the stench of misdemeanor.

Every time Blair sees Marleigh, she thinks her black hair couldn't be wound any tighter into her perfect bun, not a hair out of place. She is proven wrong time after time as the bun seems to cut off her circulation more and more each time she walks into her office.

Sadly, there is nobody else Blair could see. Marleigh has been the sole psychiatrist at Eloquoia for the past twenty years. It has been rumored that she purposely prescribes incorrect medications just so her patients could never be discharged. Some patients even report that Marleigh intentionally makes them go mad so the hospital can legally try them as "clinically insane."

"Come on, you know the drill," Kiersten replies.

Kiersten helps Blair into a new gown, black, and leads her down a long and dark corridor of rooms where patients still lie asleep. She can hear some of the patients yell out in their sleep while others seize up on their beds. Blair could hear the vibration of jerking bodies colliding with squeaky metal frames from yards away.

They continue walking until they finally reach a large wooden door, ornamented with fresh scratch marks and slow-dripping blood. Blair recalls the times when she used to claw at Gwenneth's door, crying out for painkillers when she had become addicted to Vicodin.

Soon after she had done so, she realized that she is not alone in her dying quest for meds; many other patients have also become addicted to their medications. The placebo effect has really taken a toll on them.

Kiersten knocks on the door as Blair chuckles at the sign. Marleigh Gwenneth's name had been vandalized with profanity and blasphemy.

"Enter," Blair hears Gwenneth announce from the other side.

Gwenneth's office is the most lavish room in the entire building. The walls are painted royal blue and plastered with trophies and certificates, most of which Blair questions are real. Her chair and desk are made from the finest wood, and she has more paintings and useless paperweights in her office than Blair could count.

"Sit," Doctor Gwenneth orders as Kiersten slowly backs out of the office.

"No, thanks, I'd rather stand," Blair retorts as she dreads the old wooden chair that always gives her splinters.

"I said, sit!" Gwenneth commands again, her voice so vulgar it reverberates down the halls.

Frightened, Blair carefully inches herself onto the chair, cautious to not prick herself on any broken pieces of wood.

"Ouch!" Blair exclaims as she sits on one.

"Quiet!" Gwenneth shouts as she continues typing away on her keyboard.

Blair silently ponders what information Gwenneth will pull out of her this time. During their last session, she had spilled her guts out about her relationship with Aiden.

***

Aiden was Blair's boyfriend, but he dumped her right before she was admitted to Eloquoia. To this day, Blair continues to believe that their breakup was the reason she became insane, ignoring the fact that she had been in and out of psychiatric hospitals before she even met him.

Blair always had mental health issues, but they were usually manageable. When Aiden left, her mind quickly spiraled into a place where she was no longer able to control it.

Aiden and Blair had their own apartment complex in the city, back in the days when Blair still had potential for a successful future. She moved back home to her parents after Aiden found out about her torrid affair with their neighbor. Blair foolishly believed Aiden when he told her his name should be the only name on their lease.

Blair's parents wanted to supervise her so they could ensure that she wouldn't hurt herself over the breakup. Instead, Blair was able to deceive her parents into believing that she was okay and not at all suicidal.

In fact, she was so good at lying that she even tricked herself into believing that she was not mentally affected by the pain of the breakup.

Soon after moving home, memories of Aiden and their relationship began to creep inside her mind. Whenever she was alone, her thoughts wandered uncontrollably, with self-inflicted pain as the only solution.

Slowly, she felt herself losing her sanity and desperately trying to find ways to cope and remove herself from her own mind. Her nights extended longer as she worked her way through everyone in the city who displayed the slightest interest in her.

Blair had never been promiscuous before. She always saw herself as a conservative young woman who wanted to save herself for love. However, she needed a distraction from Aiden and the pain associated with love. She needed to feel like she was getting her needs met elsewhere even though they were all superficial.

She naïvely believed that rebounds could help her find the attention she was seeking. She thought she could quiet her inner demons.

Blair distinctly remembers the time she devastated her second chance with Aiden. He went over to her parents' the morning when Blair had drunkenly brought home a random man after a hard night of clubbing.

To her demise, Aiden walked in on Blair in bed with the stranger right when he was about to make peace, apologize, and repair their relationship. He dropped the roses he had bought for her on the carpet, disgusted that she had jumped into bed with someone else less than a week after their separation.

However, the strangest part of that moment was the lack of remorse or guilt that Blair felt when she was caught. She simply shrugged it off and proceeded with her promiscuity after Aiden stormed out.

To make matters worse, Blair pretended to be the victim by posting her version of their interaction on social media. She claimed that Aiden had unfairly broken up with her through text, kicked her out of her own home, and deserved to be chastised by never finding love or happiness ever again.

She manipulated all their friends into turning against him as she poured out her soul, describing her heartbreak and depression with vivid detail. Blair found pleasure in her new game of shaming Aiden for all his flaws while feigning ignorance over her own infidelity.

But Blair is not an immoral person. She is just fragmented and cracked, with more insecurities than anyone she has ever encountered. To cover them up, she resorts to manipulation, vanity, and infinite lies to always depict herself as the "victim."

She had initially done this to protect herself from her own wandering mind, but somewhere down the line, she developed an addiction to her Machiavellian actions.

***

"I can't do this. I have to go," Blair stammers as her mind quickly returns to the present.

Without waiting for Gwenneth to respond, Blair gets up from her chair and bolts out the door, gasping for air and catching her breath as she exits.

"That was fast. Is everything okay?" Kiersten questions.

"Yeah, everything's good. Dr. Gwenneth said I'm recovering well and sent me on my way," Blair fabricates without hesitation. "Can we go outside? I need some air."

"Alright, but just for a minute. You're due in group therapy."

Kiersten unchains the titanium gates and escorts Blair, who is still handcuffed, out into the garden, or what's left of it. All around her, the trees are barren, the flowers are lifeless, and the soil has been tarnished with urine and bacteria so much so that it seems like nothing will ever grow on it again.

On her left, she sees several elderly patients despondently kicking a deflated ball back and forth, and on her right, she sees doctors bickering about treatment methods and whether they are humane.

Blair walks across the cobblestone pathway with her nurse beside her when she accidentally steps on the foot of one of the senior patients.

"Ouch! Hey! Watch where you're going!" The older man shouts in discomfort.

What a decent person would have done in this case is apologize for stepping on his foot and carry on. However, Blair had withheld the angst she felt during her flashback of Aiden in Gwenneth's office rather than releasing her thoughts and as a result, took it out on the man.

"What's your problem??" Blair shouts at him.

Frightened, the man remains mute, causing Blair's temper to flare, and she resorts to kicking him on the shin.

"Speak up, you ass! Do you feel pain now? Ow! Ow!" Blair ridicules as she repeatedly kicks him. "Does it hurt now? Does it?"

"Blair, stop!" Kiersten booms as she yanks Blair away before she could cause any more damage.

Unfortunately, Blair's anger is far greater than anything anyone could ever hope to control. She wrestles away from Kiersten and continues to kick the man without stopping, even as he bleeds to death. She fights the guards who rush over to pull her away, kicking and cursing at the almost-dead man as they transport her back inside the hospital, a heavy thunderstorm brewing close behind them.

PSYCHOSIA
THE UNEXPLAINED DISORDER

CHAPTER THREE

Neglected

"Ahh! What the hell!?" Blair squeals as Kiersten pours cold water on her face the next morning.

"You wouldn't get up. Come on, it's time for your psychotherapist appointment," Kiersten defends herself, ready for the typical post-meltdown Blair routine.

"You couldn't have picked a warmer temperature?! What the hell, dude!? Now I'm all wet! How am I supposed to go to my appointment when I'm all wet with what I hope is water?"

"I'll get you a clean gown. Now come on. We're late."

They walk down yet another long and hollow hallway at the crack of dawn as Blair hears patients snoring and screaming as they sleep. This time, they arrive in front of what used to be a closet.

Since the hospital lost its funding, Eloquoia could no longer afford to build additional offices for their employees so they were forced to turn closets into offices.

Blair's psychotherapist is Xyla Birchxyn, a thoughtful woman who used to spend her youthful years as a nomad traveling across the continents. She decided to become a psychotherapist after encountering multiple countries that lacked mental health support and started a program ten years ago to bring professionals to developing countries. She is one of those rare professionals who care more about the patients than the paychecks.

"Good morning, Blair. It's so good to see you again. Come. Come on in!" Xyla welcomes Blair as she opens the door. "Please, lie down."

Blair walks over to the dark grey sofa, kicks off her white paper slippers, and lies down on the extremely uncomfortable surface.

"How are you doing today, Blair?" Xyla asks as she rests on her bohemian-style floor pillow.

Xyla believes that centering herself close to the ground helps her connect better with her patients, creating the metaphor that she is not above them and that she understands their pain.

"Fine," Blair responds as she stares up at the dim light that hangs above her head.

She can hear her own heartbeat in the stillness as the room resounds. "Fine" is usually what patients say when they don't want to be authentic about their feelings or when they don't want to speak. Luckily, Xyla knows about "fine" and never acknowledges that as an answer.

"I know you're not fine. Tell me how you really feel. I can sit here all day until you spill."

Blair abhors being asked that question. "Feel." What does that mean anyway? Does it really matter how she feels? 'Feelings are always fluctuating anyway, so what's the point of talking about them if they're just going to be different in an hour?'

***

Blair also loathes that question because her mother always drilled her with it. When Aiden left, her mother knew the devastation would drive Blair off the rails because Blair loved him. Her whole family loved Aiden; he was part of their family, and they all assumed Aiden would be her husband one day.

When Blair first moved back home, both her parents and her brother were warm, hospitable, and supportive. As the days went by and as Blair began acting out more and more, her family found it difficult to continue trying to help someone who refused to help herself.

Still, her mother continued to hold on. Despite her self-destructive behaviors, her mother still saw Blair as the "little girl" who deserved unlimited affection and encouragement. She defended Blair's erratic behaviors by calling them "temporary" and a "phase."

She refused to believe that there was anything wrong with her daughter and always criticized others for instigating her reckless and detrimental behaviors. She refused to hold her only daughter accountable for her heinous crimes.

Her father, on the other hand, thought Blair should be thrown in prison after she nearly killed her brother for telling her that there are "plenty of fish in the sea." She threatened to turn him into a fish if he spoke another cliché and threw a knife toward him. Fortunately, she missed his face, but the knife grazed his arm in the process.

Her father saw Blair as immature and irresponsible. She is a grown woman in her twenties. She should not be getting drunk every night and whoring herself off to people she did not even know. He ordered Mrs. Pevensie to stop giving Blair an allowance because Blair always spent it on alcohol and cigarettes.

However, Mrs. Pevensie continued to do so because she could not bear to see Blair potentially get into trouble with no money to bail herself out.

Despite her mother's overprotection, her father believed that all Blair needed was some tough love. Her father is old-fashioned and constantly tells Blair that she is throwing her life down the toilet by marking her territory as the town prostitute and drunk.

Instead, she should get a job and settle down like a normal adult. He threatened many times to throw Blair out of the house because she free-loads off her mother and never helps with the chores. Luckily for Blair, time after time, her mother bailed her out of eviction.

Soon, Blair began turning her parents against each other. They already hated each other to begin with so Blair never saw it as an issue. Her parents have quarreled and fought since the day Blair was born, roaring at each other for the inanest of things and engaging in physical battles. Her mother constantly had contusions on her arms, and her father constantly had slashes on his legs.

Sometimes, Blair wonders whether she gets her destructive behaviors from her parents. She had seen blissful families before; hers was not one of them.

Blair resented her parents for hating each other but refusing to get divorced. This infuriated Blair to the point where she tried to trick them, several times, into signing divorce papers while they were either asleep or plastered.

Unfortunately for her, her plans never worked as her father always ended up beating her instead. Blair cannot remember a time in her childhood where she felt truly loved by her parents.

Sure, they bought her materialistic things, objects she wanted, but those were usually just bribes to shut her up. They never took the time to listen to or understand her.

The lack of love and familial support triggered Blair to act out at a very young age. She reminisces a time when she was only seven and pulled a knife on her mother for questioning her about the depressive thoughts she had written in her diary. However, Blair, to this day, continues to defend herself by saying it was for self-defense.

***

"Blair! You're watching that damn TV again? Get off your lazy ass and get a damn job! One more fucking day of you being a fuck-up, and I swear I will send you and your shit packing!!" Her father, Eric, screamed at her one Wednesday afternoon.

"None of your fucking business, retard! Get off my back!" Blair retaliated.

"What did you say to me? You ungrateful bitch! I allow you to live beneath my roof! I pay your bills! What the fuck makes you think you can speak to me that way? I am your damn father, and you will respect me!" Eric screamed as he slapped Blair across the face.

Blair chortled maniacally as she spat out a loose tooth onto the carpet.

"Ha! Father? Since when have you acted like a father? You don't know me! You've never been there for me! You're a pathetic excuse for a dad!"

"Shut up!" Eric slapped his daughter once more.

"Eric, stop! Stop hitting my baby girl!" Blair's mother yelled as she rushed forward.

She grabbed Eric's arm, holding him back from injuring Blair any further.

"This is none of your business, Fiona. Stay out of it," Eric argued as he turned to Fiona and pushed her away.

"I said, stop!" Fiona retorted as she shoved Eric back.

"Look! You've been coddling her her entire life. And now look what happened! She's a loser, pathetic! She's letting her life spiral down a dark and dangerous path, and you're just letting her!"

Blair remained silent.

She secretly finds pleasure whenever her parents fight. She likes the drama that brews when she is able to turn her parents against each other, not that she ever has to work hard to do so.

"So, what if I am coddling her? She's our daughter! At least I don't beat her mercilessly!"

"Fiona! Are you blind? You can't see it! Your adult daughter is a dead-beat, living at home with no job! She should be taking care of us, not the other way around!"

"Eric, how can you say that? Blair's fragile right now. She has been through some rough times. How is she supposed to get a job, much less take care of us, when she can barely take care of herself? She's not mentally well enough to do so."

"I don't give a rat's ass about mental health. It's stupid! It's just an excuse to be lazy and a fuck-up! She spends her days whoring around and drinking. She seems perfectly healthy to me. I don't know what the hell you see, but all I see is my loser of a daughter! I spent thousands on her stupid therapy sessions just to have her waste my money by not going. She doesn't even take her medication! I don't care what you have to say about her mental health. Even if she does have a loony issue, she clearly doesn't seem to care. So, why should I? All I see is her not trying. You keep telling me she's depressed and suicidal, but people who are depressed do not go out partying every night and throwing up on my carpet! I'm tired of her bullshit nonsense!"

"You still don't get it, do you? I keep trying to explain to you that her erratic behavior is because of her mental illness. Her therapist even explained it to us during her last therapy session, but like always, you clearly didn't listen. Get it through your thick skull that she's not okay! And yelling at her nonstop sure isn't going to help make it easier for her!"

"Fiona, we all have problems. When I lost my job last month, you didn't see me prostituting myself off and drinking until my liver turned brown. We have problems, but we deal with them head on. We don't stop living. We suck it up and move on. Life is hard. It doesn't mean we get to run away from it. Having a 'mental illness' does not mean we get a free pass at life. One of these days, you'll realize that what you're doing to her is actually making her worse than she already is."

"Eric, take it back. Take it back!! I am a good mother. I am a good mother!"

Seeing her mother cry did not stir up sadness in Blair. Disturbingly, the misery of others makes her feel exultant and accomplished. Blair is always miserable and knowing that others are just as miserable as her, if not more, makes her feel better about herself in that she is not alone.

A week later, Blair came home from another hard night of partying. She had met some guys at a bar and went out with them to fool around and smoke pot, not returning home until the next morning.

Again, her behavior angered her father as she prayed for another argument between her parents. She secretly hoped that she could turn her parents against each other once and for all so she could control her mother into giving her everything she wanted.

"Blair Pevensie! Where the hell were you?" Eric shouted at Blair as he saw her carrying her shoes into the house the next morning.

"Does it matter?" Blair responded.

Without giving her father a chance to speak, she walked upstairs to her room. She had a massive hangover and did not feel like dealing with her father's lectures. Trailing into her room, she plopped onto her bed, eyes slowly closing. She could hear her parents' argument renew once more.

"Fiona, do you see her!? Do you see what's happening to her?"

"I'm not blind, Eric. Of course, I do."

"Fiona!" Eric's voice rose higher, growing louder to the point where Blair was sure the windows would begin rattling in their frame.

"Can you please stop screaming at me? You need to learn to control your anger, or it's going to kill you one of these days."

"This is not about me. This is about our daughter. She is tearing apart our lives and causing us to go bankrupt! Either you stop enabling her, or I will force her out of here by any means possible. I'm tired of watching her cut herself in her room. Do you not see how she harms herself? How in the world do you think that's fine?"

Blair's brother, Shane, had been living at home when Blair moved back in. He had been dealing with financial issues and was forced to move home for a few months to get back on his feet. However, after a couple months of the constant drama, he decided to move out sooner than planned.

Shane is much like their father. He blamed Blair time after time for acting like a brat and ruining their parents' lives. They gave her everything, including taking her to therapy and buying her everything she asked for to keep her satisfied.

Yet, she continues to act ungrateful, and he could not help but resent her for their parents arguing every night, for their father drinking nonstop, and for their domestic abuse.

Nevertheless, Blair's destructive behaviors do not lie just within her family; she acts erratic around everyone she encounters. She has become so good at faking her true life and concealing her problems that even she no longer recognizes who she is.

Blair had many moments and did many things that she is not proud of, things she never thought she would do, including sleeping with her best friend's boyfriend.

To this day, she still swears it was an accident, that she had met him while she was drunk and had no recollection of what she was doing. She swore to her friend, Vanessa, that he came onto her, felt her up, and took advantage of her when she was vulnerable and unconscious.

But Blair knows there's much more to the story. When Vanessa first showed her a picture of Mark, she instantly became enamored. She thought he was the most gorgeous man she had ever laid eyes on. She wanted him badly. For weeks, she had pretended to be interested in Vanessa's relationship just so she could learn more about Mark and his daily routine.

One afternoon at the gym, she took Vanessa's phone from her duffel bag and looked up Mark's number and home address. Then she searched for his social media, catfished him for months by pretending to be a Russian transfer student, Svetlana, who craved the body of an American man, and arranged it so Vanessa would catch him in the act of cyber-cheating.

Blair originally had the plan of making her move on Mark, the vulnerable newly-heartbroken Mark, after Vanessa had broken up with him. And her plan would have been perfect, if she had not forgotten to lock her phone.

Vanessa had picked up Blair's phone, thinking it was her own when it rang, and saw a message from Mark calling her "Svetlana." That was when she pieced everything together and realized that Blair had been pretending to be Svetlana this whole time. Since that moment, Vanessa swore she would never speak to Blair again.

Vanessa had been Blair's best friend since they were five. They did everything together, including braid each other's hair and had endless slumber parties. However, when Vanessa left, Blair felt nothing. No remorse. No guilt. No melancholy.

She should have experienced agony and wrath from the loss of her one and only friend, but she didn't, almost as if she just didn't care. She just stood there, apathetic and paralyzed, as Vanessa tore up the pictures of them together in front of her and stormed out the door.

'Whatever, I didn't like her that much anyway,' Blair thought to herself. 'I'm fine without her. Who needs a friend anyway? As long as I have my booze, I'm more than happy.'

And with that self-reassurance, Blair felt a single tear trickle down her cheek.

***

"Blair?" Xyla asks, bringing Blair back into her office.

"What? Yeah, I'm fine. Fine," Blair answers.

"You dozed off again," Xyla informs her.

"What? No, I didn't," Blair refutes as she has a long history of denial.

"Okay, you didn't. What did I say?"

"Um…something about how your husband cheated on you and your kids hate you."

"Blair, you need to stop falling asleep every time you come in here. I can't help you get out of here if you don't stay awake."

Unsurprisingly, Blair's memories sparked her ire, and she begins to flare up again without a cause. Her hands clench and unclench repeatedly on her lap.

"Well, why the fuck do you make these chairs so fucking comfortable if you don't want people falling asleep in them?!" Her voice rises as her hands tighten into fists once more.

Blair's entire body feels like it is quivering. Xyla can see the fury and flame begin to form in Blair's eyes. She can tell that Blair is on the verge of another mental breakdown as this happens quite often during her therapy sessions.

"I'm so sick and tired of people accusing me of shit I'm not even doing! I'm tired of being asked how I feel all the time! I'm stuck in this hell house! So please, tell me, how am I supposed to fucking feel?"

"Blair, please, calm down," Xyla speaks softly, trying to calm Blair down before she gets even worse.

But it's too late. Blair snatches the small stainless-steel scissors off Xyla's desk and mutilates her long beautiful locks with them. Within seconds, she looks like she had just put her head through a lawnmower.

"Fine? Fine? Do I look fine now?" Blair laughs as she continues to ruin her hair.

"Help! Help! I need backup now!" Xyla yells into her phone.

Xyla never had to use her phone as much as she has when she started seeing Blair. She cannot remember a single session where she didn't have to call in the security guards to help her calm Blair down.

Blair lunges toward Xyla, scissors pointed at her neck just as the security guards swarm the room. Fortunately, before Blair could meet her target, the guards pierce her to the ground and confiscate the scissors. Any second later, and the scissors would have ended up buried deep in Xyla's neck.

She eluded the bullet this time, but she still has the scars from her last session with Blair. She feels her left elbow, her fingers tracing the raised markings. Blair had mauled her when she tried to offer consolation after Blair began crying over the loss of her relationship. Xyla had to learn the hard way to stay away from Blair's personal space.

"No! Let go of me! I'm fine! Let me go! Let me go!" Blair shrieks as one of the guards handcuffs her.

Kiersten walks in and sees Blair in tears. Her heart breaks as she hears Xyla order the guards to take her back to her cell. Kiersten hates seeing Blair in discomfort. She sees her as her own daughter and believes that Blair has so much more potential and life in her than the hospital gives her credit for.

"Kiersten, give Blair some time alone. She seemed to have a rough flashback this time. I think some time alone without distraction will be good for her. She needs to be in a safe place where she can't hurt herself or others. Her cell, alone, is the best place for that. You can check in on her in a few hours. Talk to her. See how she's holding up. She should be calmer and more receptive by then," Xyla communicates to Kiersten as she treads away.

Conversely, unbeknownst to both Kiersten and Xyla, Blair's cell is the most dangerous place in the entire hospital. Blair has become an expert at constructing razor blades from the wires in her bed, using them to cut herself daily. She hides her scars and wounds by injuring herself in places that are not easily visible, such as the soles of her feet and the back of her neck.

Still enraged at her thoughts and at Xyla for making the guards restrain her, Blair howls like a wounded animal. Kiersten, sitting on the opposite side of the shackled door, drops her head, filled with shame and guilt for not being able to help.

The angst overpowers Blair until she takes out a razor blade from her hair and makes a deep incision on her inner thighs. She cries out at the pain as blood surges down her legs, forming a pool beneath her.

PSYCHOSIA
THE UNEXPLAINED DISORDER

CHAPTER FOUR

Confined

"Inmates! Inmates! Time to drag your lazy asses out of bed! Line up! Shortest to tallest! Now! Now! Now! Let's go!" The prison guard, Stevens, ordered.

No one responded.

"I said, now!" Stevens shouted again, her voice thunderous throughout the prison walls.

And just like that, the prisoners sprung out of their cells and bustled to line up, some perplexed while trying to measure heights, others squirmed because they were too petrified to pee beforehand.

Ali Stevens, a former military soldier, was the toughest guard at Schannes Correctional Facility. Many feared her, prisoners and staff alike. She was known to brutally beat inmates who challenged her. She even went as far as to bite the ear off one inmate who tried to fight against her.

The inmate's ear split off, and she bled to death. However, Stevens was also known to transform even the worst criminals to civil citizens, that is, the criminals who manage to survive.

Stevens began to count the inmates, starting from top to bottom, one by one, until she came up short.

"Where the hell is Inmate 2257? Inmate 2257! Get your sorry ass down here immediately, or you will regret it!"

"I think she's still in bed," Inmate 3582 responded.

"Did I ask you to speak, Inmate 3582? You will only speak when you are spoken to. Do you understand?"

Inmate 3582 nodded, eyes wide and hands shaking, as Stevens walked over to Blair's cell.

"Inmate 2257! I am going to say this one time and one time only! Get your ass up and stand in line, or I will be forced to utilize physical force."

"No," Blair mumbled, still half asleep. "I'm not afraid of you, you disgusting old hag. No wonder you're alone."

Sergeant Stevens had a very low tolerance for disobedience, but an even lower one for disrespect. She let herself into Blair's cell and began beating her with her truncheon.

"You shall not speak to your commanding officer with such disrespect! You shall not speak to your commanding officer until you are spoken to first! You shall listen and obey when your commanding officer instructs you to!" Stevens chanted with each new strike of her truncheon.

"You're a pathetic nothing, Inmate 2257. You will forever rot in this cell and die the same way you have lived: a piece of shit," Stevens called out, spitting her gum on Blair's curled up figure before marching out of her cell.

"Bring her to the pit," Stevens ordered the other guards.

"The pit" was a room much worse than solitary confinement. There was only enough space in there for a single inmate, with barely enough room to turn around.

There were no windows, bed, or toilet inside the pit. The door to the pit was made of steel that contained a timed lock with no window slit for communication or light. Prisoners who entered the pit must remain in there for at least one week before the lock released them, that is, if someone didn't reset it first.

Prisoners inside the pit must stand in complete darkness due to the lack of space to bend over or to sit and sleep. If prisoners needed to use the toilet, they would have to do so standing up and endure their own filth for the remainder of the time.

Prisoners were devoid of all food and oxygen. Many never made it out of the pit alive. Most were found suffocated due to the lack of air inside the pit. Others were found eating their own excrement or arm, sometimes bleeding to death before they were released.

There were no medics or clinic inside Schannes. Inmates close to death were left in their cells to die, their bodies burned in the yard, and their families never notified. Blair's cell mate had accidentally punctured her ulnar artery on her bed spring, blood gushing out nonstop, but was ultimately left to bleed out and perish in her cell as guards refused to call for medical assistance.

As the guards entered Blair's cell to bring her to the pit, Blair fought back however way she could. She kicked her legs and managed to scratch and bite both guards. She screamed at the top of her lungs before being pulled down the halls of the prison and thrown into a small chamber located in the basement of the facility.

No one ever went into the basement. Most inmates feared it and referred to it as "hell." The basement was once used for storage but turned into a place for the deadliest of criminals.

However, before the guards thrusted Blair into the pit and turned on the timed lock, they ganged up on her in the basement, felt her up, and forced her to perform fellatio on them both, quickly hurling her into the pit after she decided to bite one of the guards.

Blair found herself alone in complete darkness. She could not see her own hands as she tried to feel around her, only to stop shortly at the walls she was surrounded by. She tried to turn around but became stuck as she moved.

Blair screamed, the animal-like noise reverberating off the walls. Unfortunately, there was no one around to hear her. Even if they could, no one cared. She was all alone.

Day One

"I don't know what I have done to deserve this misfortune. I have done nothing wrong, and I have only ever wanted to express my own voice. It's not my fault that people around me are too ignorant to realize the potential my opinions are capable of. I don't belong here. I don't belong here! Let me out!"

Day Two

"I didn't mean to do what I did. It was a necessity and for self-defense. I had to protect my heart, my soul! I had to protect myself from the heartache he was causing me! It's not my fault! He triggered me! It's not my fault!"

Day Three

"I'm so fucking hungry. I tried eating my own feces, but it was so disgusting that I ended up vomiting on myself. The smell. It makes it so hard to breathe. I need to get out! I need air! I want to kill myself! I can't go a second longer like this!"

Day Four

Silence.

Day Five

"This is it. This is my life. This is how I die. I am innocent of the crimes I am accused of. I don't deserve to die like this. I will forever remain a forgotten child, castrated for sins that I have not committed. I hate everyone around me. No one cares about me. Now I'm starting to not care about me either. This is the end. The end...the end..."

Day Six

Silence.
Day Seven
Silence.

PSYCHOSIA
THE UNEXPLAINED DISORDER

57

CHAPTER FIVE

Used

"Can you please pass me the red paint?" Blair gestures to Kiersten during her creative arts group therapy one morning.

Ever since the incident in her sector, Kiersten was ordered to remain by Blair's side 24/7. After failing to hear a sound from Blair's cell for over an hour, Kiersten walked in to find Blair blacked out and bleeding on the cold asphalt ground.

"Sure. Here you go," Kiersten responds as she hands Blair the small jar of acrylic red paint.

Half-restrained, Blair struggles to grab hold of the jar from Kiersten's hand. Her arms are tightly bound to her sides with only her hands moving freely.

"Thanks."

Staring at the blank piece of cardstock paper in front of her, Blair takes her thin brush, dips it into the paint, and begins to draw.

"What are you painting?" Kiersten asks, looking over Blair's shoulder.

"Love," Blair calmly responds.

Kiersten looks at Blair's art and sees black hearts outlined with cracks and blood, decorated with possessed demons emerging from them as she writes "Aiden, my love" on the corner of the paper.

"Do you like it?" Blair asks as she smiles mischievously at Kiersten.

Kiersten smiles back, trying hard to hold back her appalled reaction. Blair is an incredible artist, able to create pieces far beyond imagination. When she isn't in anguish, she has the stroke of angels. The hospital even enlisted her to paint their mural of peace and hope before she became manic.

Now, she only seems to find pleasure in drawing images of hate, blood, and the terrors inside her, a talent Kiersten believes she is wasting.

***

Blair loved to paint as a child. She had won countless awards from art competitions for her surreal depictions of the human mind. As a teenager, she sold many of her works to galleries and was named "National Artist of the Year" for five consecutive years. However, all that changed when she met Aiden.

Aiden and Blair met at a local art club near her hometown. One day, while Blair was deep into her painting strokes of the nude model in front of her, she heard a soft and deep voice from behind.

"Beautiful. A work of art."

Blair turned around and saw a young man wearing a scarf and fedora standing behind her, grinning.

"Oh yeah, she's gorgeous. I wish I could look like her," Blair responded.

"No, not her. Your painting. It's stunning. You're really good!"

Blair was taken back by surprise as she thought, 'Who is this man, and why is he complimenting me?'

Startled and anxious, with sweat trickling down her temple, she opened her mouth to speak, with barely any sound coming out.

"I...I...I'm fine."

"Fine? What do you mean?" The strange man asked.

"Shit. I'm sorry. I meant to say 'thank you'," Blair corrected herself, now ashamed and embarrassed. "Excuse me, I have to go."

Blair got up to leave but quickly realized that she was not going anywhere. The man had grabbed her arm and held her back.

"My name's Aiden. Hi!" He said.

"Hi...I'm Blair," Blair responded meekly.

"Blair! I like that! My mom's name is Blair too."

"Really?" Blair questioned with disbelief.

"No, I don't know why I said that. I thought it would impress you. Now I realize it sounded creepy."

Blair chuckled.

"So, what brings you here? I haven't seen you around before."

"What do you mean? I come here all the time."

"Oh," he laughed, a hand reaching up to scratch the back of his neck. "I meant, I haven't seen you around because I don't come here often. I'm only here because I heard they were featuring a naked...anyway! What brings you here?"

"I come here all the time to paint. It relaxes me."

"That's awesome! Are you an artist?"

"No. I just like to paint."

"That's awesome! I wish I was artistic. All I can draw are stick figures. Hey, listen. Do you want to get out of here? Grab a drink or something?"

'What the hell?' Blair thought to herself. 'Who the hell is this kid, and why won't he leave me alone? No, I don't want to get a drink with you. I don't care how cute you are. You're creepy.'

"Sorry, I can't. I need to finish this," Blair declined.

"Alright, suit yourself."

Aiden strolled away, and just when Blair began feeling relieved that he was no longer bothering her, he returned minutes later with a cocktail in each hand.

"You look like a rum and coke kind of gal," Aiden said as he plopped himself down on the chair next to her.

Slightly annoyed, Blair pretended not to notice him. 'Maybe if I ignore him long enough, he'll get the hint and go away.'

Her plan backfired.

"Well, since you couldn't go grab a drink with me, I brought the drink to you," Aiden said smugly.

"Thanks, but I don't want it," Blair replied, a frown crossing her face.

"Alright, more for me then. Two drinks and some beautiful art. A guy can't ask for better than that!" Aiden cheered.

"Can you just go away, please? You're really distracting, and I'm trying to finish this."

Blair was fed up with Aiden's constant pestering. She had come to the club to get away from her family because they constantly annoyed her with questions. Now, she discovered that her "peaceful spot" had become more menacing.

"Geez. Who put a thorn on your chair? Fine, I'll leave. Cheers!" Aiden waved as he stood up and skipped away with his empty glasses.

And with that, Blair believed she would never have to see or deal with Aiden ever again. She walked out of the club an hour later and drove home. But for some reason, she couldn't get the man out of her mind. She pictured him as she climbed into bed, forcing herself to watch a movie to get him out of her head before she quickly fell asleep.

Hours later, she was awoken by the sound of her phone beeping.

'Who the fuck is texting me this late?' Blair questioned as she reached toward her nightstand for her phone

Unknown: Hey, Blair! It's Aiden! Remember me?

'Aiden?' Blair thought. 'Is this kid fucking stalking me?'

Blair: How'd you get this number?

Aiden: Oh! I probably should have mentioned! My friend, Alex, owns the club that you go to. I got it from her. Hope you don't mind.

Blair: Don't mind!? Of course, I mind! Are you stalking me? Why won't you leave me alone?!

Aiden: I'm sorry. I tried, but I couldn't. You intrigue me, and I want to get to know you more. I'm sorry if I seemed creepy doing so, but sometimes I come on too strong, as you may have noticed.

Blair: What would it take for you to leave me alone?

Aiden: One date. Let me take you out tomorrow night. One date. If you still hate me after, I promise I'll leave you alone for good.

Blair: Fine. Good night.

Blair sent her final text and crawled back under her covers. She wasn't sure about what she had just agreed to, but at least Aiden stopped texting her. She must have done something right.

***

The next morning, Blair received another text from Aiden.

Aiden: Hey, gorgeous! Good morning! It's Aiden again!

Unbothered by his text, Blair ignored him, only to receive another one.

Aiden: Hey! Do you like ice cream? I'm thinking we could hang out at my favorite ice cream shop tonight! What do you say?

Blair: Sure, whatever.

Despite her crass response, Blair was secretly excited for her date. She acted cold toward Aiden but deep down, she liked him. No boy or man had ever paid that much attention to her, and she relished in it. She loved feeling wanted, and acting aloof seemed to work in her favor.

Blair spent the entire day getting herself ready, hitting the gym for hours, getting her hair and makeup done professionally, and she even bought a new dress, one that was sexy enough to grab his attention but not too revealing.

She didn't want to give off the wrong message. She starved herself all day to maintain her flat stomach in case anything happened with Aiden. She told herself that she wasn't that kind of person, but secretly, she loved it when men tried to sleep with her on the first date.

Ding! She heard her phone go off. It was Aiden.

Aiden: I can't wait to see you again!

Blair smiled. His message had made her subconsciously smile.

'Did I just smile? No, no, no. I can't smile. I can't like him.'

But she couldn't stop. She pulled her lip gloss out of her pocket and polished her plump lips one last time, untied her hair to let her dark locks flow down her back as she grabbed her purse, and began driving to the address that Aiden had texted her.

Aiden had offered to pick her up, but Blair couldn't have a stranger, especially one of his caliber, knowing where she lived. She needed to trust him first, so she insisted that she drove herself. That way, if anything went awry, she could just get in her car and leave.

Upon arrival, Aiden was already seated, dressed in a white buttoned-down shirt and dark blue jeans, licking a chocolate cone. He stood up quickly as he saw Blair pull up.

"Sorry, I'm late," Blair said. "Did you wait long?"

"Nope! I just got here! This ice cream is fantastic! You must try it! What do you like? My treat!"

"Just vanilla is fine. Thanks."

"I expected you to be a vanilla type of girl," Aiden said as he turned to the window. "One vanilla cone for the young lady, please."

"Thank you for the ice cream. That's really sweet of you."

"Blair, honey. You are a really lucky girl. Do you know why?"

'Honey? Why is he calling me that? I just met him,' Blair thought. 'Strange.'

"Why?" She asked.

"Because I'm a catch. Any girl would be more than lucky to go out with me, and you're lucky that I've chosen you," Aiden winked as he arrogantly grinned at Blair.

Blair thought nothing more to this other than how Aiden had a big ego. She couldn't see that his behaviors were all warning signs for her, all warning signs she disregarded that would eventually bite her in the ass.

Soon, their relationship began to progress. Blair tried to remain reserved, but she quickly scrapped that as she jumped right into a hotel bed with Aiden later that night. She could not explain it, but there was something about him that made her throw away her beliefs and follow her instincts.

Maybe he had cast some sort of spell over her. Maybe he was just that charismatic. Or maybe she was ravenous for human touch and affection since her last boyfriend ran off on her that she was desperate enough to be with any man.

Aiden was, or at least appeared like, everything Blair had ever wanted in a partner. He constantly gave her his undivided attention, bought her gifts, and always paid for her when they went out on dates, never complaining and never asking for anything in return. The only request he ever had was for Blair to provide affection and love when affection and love were well-deserved.

***

A year later, Aiden asked Blair to move in with him.

"We should look for a place together. Something we both like, and we can split the rent. That way, we can call the place 'ours' and make our relationship official," Aiden told Blair.

Blinded by "love," Blair willingly agreed.

"That sounds like an amazing idea! I love you so much! You always come up with the best ideas, and you're always there for me. I'm so happy with you!"

"I'm so happy with you too, Blair! Hey, listen, work hasn't been going so well for me lately. Half my department just got laid off because our company is downsizing. Would you mind covering the first couple months until I can find a second job and pay you back what I owe?"

Blair never lived on her own before. Up until then, she lived with her parents and had no idea the struggles that came with paying rent and utilities.

"Of course! I can take care of it. No problem!" Blair responded without taking a moment to consider the consequences.

"Thank you so much, babe! You're the best!" Aiden grinned as he kissed her on the cheek.

Living with Aiden felt like a whole new world. For the first time in a long time, Blair saw hope in her life because her relationship with Aiden had pulled her out of her drunken nights.

She believed that he helped her become an improved person. Before Aiden, Blair did not have boundaries. She did not have self-respect. Aiden changed all that for her. Aiden was the fairytale prince she had always wanted.

However, soon things began to change. Aiden had turned from being sweet and sensitive to being cold and indifferent.

"Hey, honey. What do you want for dinner?" Blair asked Aiden as she walked into the apartment after a long day at work one day.

"Oh, I ate already," Aiden responded without taking his eyes off the television.

"I'm sorry. What was that?" Blair asked again, distracted.

"I made dinner already," Aiden replied again, pointing to the pile of dirty dishes and pans on the stove and in the sink.

"Oh, cool. Where's mine?" Blair glanced around for a plastic-wrapped plate of food.

"I didn't make yours."

"Why not? I always make extra for you when I cook."

"I didn't know when you were coming home."

"I come home the same time every day. Why would you think I didn't need dinner?"

Aiden grew heated. He was trying to watch the game on TV, but Blair refused to stop interrogating him about something as frivolous as dinner.

"Look! You're a grown woman. You know how to cook for yourself. I don't need to baby you all the time!"

Blair was taken back, but she tried to understand and push past it.

"Okay, fine. I'll make my own food. Can you at least clean up your mess so I can use the pan? You used up everything that was clean."

"I'll get to it later."

"Can you please do it now? I'm hungry."

"Blair! Can you stop!? I'm busy here! If you want them cleaned, you clean them. Stop making me do all your shitty work for you!" Aiden shouted before turning back toward the TV, refusing to converse with Blair the rest of the night.

Hysterical and baffled over what had just happened, Blair began to feel almost an itch that there was something wrong with their relationship. A part of her knew she had to leave, but the stronger side of her was compelling her to stay because she believed that she loved Aiden.

***

Over the course of the next few months, Aiden's behavior took a turn for the worse. The promise that Aiden had made before they moved in continued to fall through month after month. They moved into their apartment over six months ago, and Blair had yet to see him pull his part of the rent.

One day, while Blair was running errands and doing their weekly grocery shopping, she ran into Aiden's parents.

"Hello, Mr. and Mrs. Mzithial! It's such a coincidence running into you two here! I didn't know you shopped here," Blair exclaimed.

"Blair! It's so good to see you again! How are things going with Aiden? We haven't spoken to him in a while, but we have heard great things about the two of you together. You two are too cute!" Mrs. Mzithial's face brightened with a wide smile, the corners of her eyes wrinkling.

"Good to see you, Blair! My wife and I are visiting friends in the area for a housewarming and, silly us, we forgot to buy a gift, so we came here to quickly pick something out," Mr. Mzithial added.

"Good! Things are good! Aiden and I are doing well, and we're really happy together. You two have such a great son!" Blair responded pretentiously.

"Oh, sweetie! We need to go," Mrs. Mzithial said as she glanced at her watch. "It was good running into you, Blair! Say 'hi' to Aiden for me, and tell him to call us!"

"Sure thing, Mrs. Mzithial! Enjoy your housewarming! Bye, Mr. Mzithial!" Blair waved as Aiden's parents elatedly skipped out the door.

'They have been married for over thirty years and are still as happy as ever. I wish I had that,' Blair sighed.

She felt blameworthy for lying to the Mzithials about her relationship with Aiden. But, then again, she couldn't bad mouth Aiden in front of his own parents; that would make her look like the devil.

"Blair, I can't pay rent this month. I still don't have the money. I'm sorry. My um…parents had an emergency and needed my help," Aiden called out as Blair walked through the door.

He was lounging around in his underwear and eating take-out sushi.

'Liar! You're a fucking liar!' Blair wanted to scream.

"Really? What happened?" Blair knew Aiden was lying, but she was also curious to hear his concocted story.

"My father just called from the hospital. They were in a car accident, and my mother is seriously injured. They are struggling with getting the money they need for their medical bills and asked me to help. I'm sorry, Blair. I wanted to help you with rent, I really did, but this was an emergency. You understand, right?" He didn't quite meet her eyes as he spoke, instead, remained intensely focused on his sushi.

'I understand that you're a pathetic loser and a liar!' Blair wanted to shriek. 'How dare he lie to her, especially about something as drastic as his parents getting injured? More importantly, where the hell is all his money going?'

Nevertheless, Blair continued to let his excuses pass to avoid stirring up further drama and pain. Aiden was not the easiest person to talk to, and any form of confrontation would cause him to explode at her and walk out the door. He lied about being laid off from his job when he had quit instead, and several times, she had walked in on him stealing from her.

However, she continued to justify to herself that Aiden was just going through a rough time and needed her to be patient until he could get back on his feet.

***

Over the next several weeks, Blair became irrationally suspicious of Aiden, suspecting that he was cheating on her even though she didn't have the evidence. She looked through his phone to see if she could catch him in the act, but unfortunately, she came up short.

"He has to be cheating on me," Blair told herself one day as she stared in her mirror. "He's acting distant, and he always leaves the apartment at odd hours."

Still, because Blair did not have evidence, she had to create her own proof to catch Aiden in the act. So, she bought a new phone and generated her own alias, Veronica Valz, to try to see if Aiden would fall for her bait so Blair could catch him in the act of infidelity.

Veronica: I had a great time last night! I can't wait to see you again!

Aiden: I'm sorry. Who is this?

Veronica: It's me! Vicky! Remember, we went out to that club last night and did some things in my car afterward? You told me how much you loved kissing my luscious breasts.

Aiden: I'm sorry, you must have me confused with someone else.

Veronica: Is this Dean?

Aiden: No, sorry. My name is Aiden. I'm afraid whoever this Dean guy is gave you the wrong number.

Veronica: Oh my gosh! I'm so sorry! I feel so stupid! He seemed like a perfectly decent man. I let him do things to me that I never even dreamt of! I'm so foolish!

Aiden: I'm sorry.

Veronica: Hey, Aiden, right? Do you know why guys treat women like shit? Like, why would he do that to me?

Aiden: I don't know. I'm sure you'll find a decent guy someday.

Veronica: Aiden, do you have a girlfriend?

Aiden: Um...sort of. We're not on great terms right now.

Veronica: Aw, why not?

Aiden: I'm sorry. It's kind of personal.

Veronica: Come on, you can talk to me about it. I won't judge. I promise.

Aiden: Nah, I kind of just want to forget about it.

Veronica: So, you mean like a distraction?

Aiden: Yeah, exactly. I've been doing that lately. Going out at night with my friends and just getting drunk. Nothing too serious.

Veronica: Well, maybe I can help you out a bit.

Aiden: What do you mean?

Moments later, Aiden received an image of bare breasts, which Blair had found on the Internet.

Veronica: Those are my luscious breasts, Aiden. Do you like them?

Aiden: Yeah, they're nice.

Veronica: Do you wish you could touch them?

Before Aiden could decide on his next answer, Blair walked in, slamming the door. Aiden quickly closed his phone and threw it on the coffee table, thinking he had saved himself as he greeted Blair at the door.

"Hey, honey! It's a beautiful day out! Let's go for a walk around the park nearby!" Aiden said unusually cheerfully.

"That sounds like a great idea. Hey, can you make me some coffee? I'm feeling really tired."

"Sure, honey."

As Aiden waltzed into the kitchen to make the coffee, Blair shouted, "I wonder if it's going to rain today!"

She picked up Aiden's phone, pretending to check the weather while fully knowing what she was about to do.

Since she had been pretending to be Vicky, she knew she could finally catch Aiden in the act of adultery.

"Aiden! Who is she!?" Blair screamed as Aiden walked back in from the kitchen with a hot cup of coffee.

"Nobody," Aiden answered with a shrug of his shoulders as Blair showed him the photo of "Vicky's breasts."

"She sure doesn't look like 'nobody'. Her boobs look like you're cheating on me!"

Blair pinched herself on the small of her back so she could force herself to cry without Aiden noticing.

By this point, Blair expected Aiden to confess to his betrayal and apologize. However, he refused to stand down and stirred up the quarrel even more.

"Does it matter? What I do with my time is none of your business! Besides, you don't ever pay attention to me anymore, and when you do, you just blame me for stupid shit like not washing the dishes. You're rarely home, and whenever I want sex, you claim you're 'too tired'. What the fuck do you expect me to do? Just wait around for you when I get nothing in return?"

"I'm barely home because I have a job I need to go to! Excuse me for not catering to your every need! I support us. That doesn't give you an excuse to sleep with other women. Unlike you, I don't make up excuses to cover up not having a job just so I can sleep around with other people! I'm so sick of supporting a loser and a child! I hate you! I hate you!"

Antagonism flushed over Blair. She had never felt this irate before in her life, and she wanted the excruciating pain inside her head to just go away. She didn't have the means or strength to handle this sort of anger. Her eyes felt like they were on fire, and her skin felt like it was blistering.

Without thinking, she reached out her hand and struck Aiden across the face so hard that his nose began to bleed and his face became inflamed.

"Oh my god! Aiden, baby! I'm so sorry! I didn't mean to hurt you. I was just mad at the whole situation, and my anger just came out. I really didn't mean it! I'm so, so sorry! Can you please forgive me?" Blair rushed to Aiden and apologized over and over again as soon as she realized what had happened.

"Get away from me, you psychopath!" Aiden pushed Blair to the ground and stormed out of the apartment, leaving Blair in tears.

Still traumatized at what had happened, Blair began to immediately fault herself for Aiden walking out. She blamed herself for striking Aiden and for starting an argument with him when they were supposed to go for a stroll in the park.

She blamed herself for Aiden cheating on her and told herself that she deserved it. She also blamed herself for Aiden abandoning his job because she had made him too stressed out at home to focus on work.

But worst of all, she blamed herself for allowing this situation to happen, this situation where she was unsure of whether to stay or leave, of whether to keep going or end her life. She blamed herself for being alive.

'Maybe if I had just paid more attention to him instead of going to work, he would have stayed. Maybe if I hadn't nitpicked on every little thing, he would not have gotten angry and left. Maybe I should have shown him more love and attention when I noticed that he was drifting away. Maybe I should have catered to him more so he felt loved and cared for. Maybe I should have never gotten into this relationship. Maybe then I wouldn't have ruined it. Maybe then I wouldn't have ruined his life. Maybe then I wouldn't have ruined my life. Maybe then. Just maybe.'

And with this menacing thought, Blair walked into the kitchen, pulled out a sharp knife from the drawer, and impulsively stabbed the palm of her right hand.

PSYCHOSIA
THE UNEXPLAINED DISORDER

CHAPTER SIX

Murdered

"So, how are you feeling today, Blair?" Adelaide Myniski asks.

After the episode with Blair, Xyla handed in her two-weeks' notice. She had become so fed up with Blair's outbursts that she decided to return to her nomadic life, assisting the mental health of those she encounters on the road.

In her place is Adelaide, a stern and neurotic young woman who recently received her master's in mental health, specializing in the criminal and the psychotic.

"Who the hell are you? Are you even a doctor? You look younger than me. Kiersten! I want out of here! I don't want this child dictating whether I get out of here!"

"Blair, you need to calm down. I am more than qualified to do this job, and I am here to help you."

"What do you know anyway?"

"I graduated top of my class at Hyntsynger University. I have been professionally trained in this field, and I have a certified license. I can help you, Blair. Please let me help you so you can get your life back."

"Fuck you. I have a life. I want to leave," Blair replies.

"You will be able to leave after we are done with our session. Now, please tell me, how are you feeling today?"

Blair stammers under her breath, barely loud enough for Adelaide to hear.

"I'm sorry. What was that?" Adelaide asks.

Blair stammers under her breath again, this time even more faint than the previous.

"Blair, you need to speak up. I can't hear a word you're saying. How are you feeling?"

"I'm fine, just fucking fine! You hear me now!? I'm fucking fine. Don't you people have anything better to do than ask me how I'm feeling all the time? God! Leave me alone! Leave us alone! Nobody wants you here!" Blair fumes as she gets up from the sofa and begins walking out the door.

"Blair, stop! Where are you going? You can't leave! We're not done with our session!" Adelaide calls from behind her.

"Back to my room. I hate you. You're stupid," Blair replies as she waves her middle finger in the air.

"Come back here, young lady! We are not done!"

"Young lady? Really? I'm older than you! What are you, like twelve?"

"I...," Adelaide begins to speak.

"Nope! Not another word! We're done here. Thank you for wasting my time."

"Blair!"

Vexed, Blair pulls the razor blade out of her hair, pushes Adelaide against the wall, and touches the blade to her throat.

"Listen, woman. One more word out of you, and I will cut your carotid artery so deep you'd wish you were never born."

Blair's cognizance recognizes that she needs to put the blade down and apologize to Adelaide for threatening her, but every time she tries to tell herself to, her body refuses to listen. She voices to her mind to stop and put the blade down, but her arm refuses to budge.

All she can feel and hear are the constant buzzing inside her head, compelling her thoughts to spiral erratically, only stopping when she sees the door bust open and her old friends, the security guards, rushing in and aiming a rifle at her.

"Let her go, Blair! Put the blade down and let her go. Don't make me shoot you!" Kotar, the head security guard, shouts.

Still holding the blade, Blair begins to weep. "I just want to go home! I just want to go home!"

"I said, put the blade down! Don't make me say it again, Blair!" Kotar reiterates.

Slowly and frighteningly, Blair pulls the blade away from Adelaide's neck. As soon as she does so, the guards quickly seize her and restrain her on the ground.

"I just want to go home. I just want to go home," Blair cries out again, unaware of what's going on around her.

"Come on, Blair. Let me take you back to your room," Kiersten says as she reaches for Blair's arm.

"Ow! Ow! Ow! You're hurting me! Stop! Stop touching me!"

"Blair, I'm not hurting you. I'm barely touching you. Come on, let's head back."

"No! Let me go! Let me go! I don't want to go with you! You're trying to hurt me! Don't let her take me!"

Blair continues to scream as the guards drag her to her cell, kicking and crying as she is being pulled down the hall while the other patients stare in ignorance.

"Stop staring at me! Stop looking at me! You don't know me! You don't know me!"

Upon reaching Blair's vault, Kiersten unshackles the door, and the guards heave her inside, confining her in behind them as Blair continues to cry.

"I just want to go home. I just want to go home!" Blair sniffles as she sits on the ground of her cell…alone.

***

Later that night, Kiersten lets herself into Blair's chamber.

"Come on, Blair. You've been held up in your room all week. The other patients are having a movie night in the cafeteria. I think you should join them. Socialize a bit. Get to know the other residents. Stop being anti-social," Kiersten tells Blair.

Defeated and depleted, Blair unenthusiastically agrees and walks down the hall with Kiersten to the cafeteria. The movie being played is "One Beautiful Victim," one of Blair's favorite movies of all time.

She enters the cafeteria to find some of the staff trying to get the movie to work. The DVD player has a glitch, and they need to fix it before they could play the movie. The patients are getting anxious, so the nurses decide to put the news on to distract them while they fix the problem.

"This is ridiculous. The movie doesn't even work," Blair mumbles as she turns around and proceeds to head back to her quarters.

However, she suddenly hears an announcement that stops her from moving.

"Earlier this morning, 30-year-old Bill Tyler was found murdered in his apartment. Investigators discovered his body covered in blood on his bed after they received an anonymous phone call and have suspicions that his ex-girlfriend, Kyllie Mox, may be the suspect. Police are currently investigating the scene and questioning several residents in the apartment building. More to come later tonight." The news station's jingle blares after the anchorman signs off.

"Ah, got it!" One of the nurses announce as she pops the movie in.

However, Blair could not focus on watching what is playing on the screen. The news made her consciousness flash back to the nightmare she had been trying to hide ever since she was admitted into Eloquoia.

Eloquoia is no ordinary psychiatric hospital. Eloquoia is reserved as the psychiatric hospital for the dangerously deranged. Only criminals who have been diagnosed with serious mental illnesses are admitted. Blair hates acknowledging that she is a criminal, a dangerous murderer, but it is true.

Blair was admitted to Eloquoia Psychiatric Hospital because she had murdered Aiden.

***

When Blair was forced to move back to her parents after being kicked out of her apartment by Aiden, she hated every fiber of his being and swore to herself that she would never think about or talk to him ever again. He had taken everything from her, used her, and broke her heart.

However, as time passed, she realized how much she missed him and wanted to see and kiss him again. She stalked his social media activity and noticed that he was still listed as "in a relationship" with her. This made her smile. Maybe he still loved her. Maybe there was still hope for them.

She needed to know. She needed to know whether he still wanted to be with her or whether he had moved on. Over the next few weeks, she aggressively continued to stalk his profile, making sure that he did not get into another relationship.

Whenever his profile status changed to "dating," Blair stalked the women and persuaded them to leave him or break up with him by feeding them lies about how he was either sadistic or had an STD. Aiden never found out why all his dates began cancelling on him. He never linked it back to Blair. He never even knew that Blair had been watching him.

Blair then came across a post from Aiden saying he was going to spend his 30th birthday by the lake to test out his new boat.

"This is perfect. I'll buy him some brand-new boat shoes and wish him 'happy birthday'. Maybe I can make up an excuse that I was just going for a run in the area and 'accidentally' run into him. This is perfect!" Blair cheerfully exclaimed to herself.

Blair spent that morning buying a new outfit for her "casual run." She needed something racy but also sent the message that she "just threw it on." She found a revealing hot pink sports bra and thin spandex shorts that left her buttocks hanging out.

She also bought the most expensive pair of boat shoes she could find to try to entice Aiden into getting back together with her. She then grabbed a knife and engraved a mini heart on her wrist with the initials "EP & AM" next to it to symbolize her eternal love with Aiden.

That night, Blair's plan was going smoothly. She placed Aiden's present in the trunk of her car and drove to the lake. She then used her binoculars to track Aiden down and ran toward his direction, casually bumping into him.

"Oh my god! Aiden! What a coincidence! I did not expect to see you here!" Blair exclaimed.

"Blair? What are you doing here? Did you know I was going to be here?" Aiden asked suspiciously.

"What!? Don't be silly! Of course not! I was just going for my evening run and bumped into you! How have you been?"

"Good...?"

"That's awesome! I've been doing amazing too! Working out a lot. My boobs are definitely getting more defined, and my butt is getting bigger," Blair boasted, her voice purred as she tried to entice Aiden. "Oh my gosh! It's your birthday today, isn't it? Happy Birthday!!

Speaking of birthday, I have your present that I bought for you while we were still together. I can't return it, and it's not my size, so I might as well give it to you before it goes to waste. Wait here, let me go get it!" Blair sprinted off to her car, making sure she added an extra bounce in her steps so she could dangle her ass and hair in front of Aiden as she skipped.

To her surprise, when Blair returned, she was startled to see a woman hugging Aiden. Furious, she stormed over to them.

"Aiden, who the hell is this? Is this your new girlfriend?"

"Not that it's any of your business, but no. This is my friend, Alex. I've known her since we were kids. Alex, this is Blair," Aiden responded.

"Hi, Blair! It's so nice to meet you! I have heard so much about you. Say, Blair, Aiden and I are just about to take the boat out into the water. Would you like to join us? I'm sure there's enough room in the boat for one more!" Alex said cheerfully.

"No, it's okay. I'm fine. I don't like sailing that much. You two go ahead. I'll hang around here until you get back," Blair responded sarcastically as she darted sharp stares toward Alex, who began walking off with Aiden, jumping on his back and wrestling him as they walked toward his boat.

"Friend, my ass. She doesn't look like just his friend to me," Blair grumbled under her breath as she became envious of Alex, with her beautiful blonde hair and long thin legs. "It's sickening."

Without noticing, Blair began to cry, her tears dripping into the sand as she dropped her present for Aiden and began to lose hope of ever being with Aiden again. All those weeks she had spent stalking him, had spent elated over the thought of being with him again, quickly seemed to wash away in the waves as her future husband walked off with another woman.

The sun was beginning to set, and the wind began to pick up. Aiden and Alex were still out on the water, laughing with and embracing each other under the starry sky.

'It's okay,' Blair assured herself. 'They're just friends. They're just friends. I still have a chance.'

Suddenly, Blair saw Aiden lean over and kiss Alex on the lips, his arms wrapped around her, and their bodies close together.

Blair saw Alex kiss him back passionately as Aiden reached his hand under her bikini top and leaned her down onto the deck of the boat. Minutes later, she saw Aiden get up, take his shirt off, and lean back down toward Alex.

Blair screamed, loud enough for the pigeons to fly away but not enough for Aiden and Alex to hear her.

Blair continued to sit by the lake, staring at Aiden and Alex fornicating over the next several hours. She could not believe what she was seeing. They both had lied to her right in front of her face.

Panic began to devastate her. The only thing that would've eased Blair's mind was making up with Aiden and being with him again. Now that he was with someone else, anxiety began to rush over Blair as she became confused and unsure as to how to recover from her pain.

Then she realized something. Aiden was the source of all her pain. He pushed his way into her life, fucked it up, and now he's literally killing her by fucking some other woman right in front of her. He truly was the devil.

"Aiden needs to die," Blair found herself whispering subconsciously.

There was no time to concoct a plan. There was no turning back. There was no time to think through whether this was a reasonable idea. She had to do it. She had to get it over with. She had to murder Aiden.

Blair's thoughts were distracted as she watched Aiden and Alex come back to shore. Alex finished tying up her bikini top and gave Aiden one last kiss before heading off in the opposite direction. Blair's scour quickly turned into a grin as she saw Aiden running toward her.

"Still here? Isn't it getting kind of late for you?" Aiden asked as he saw Blair still sitting on the sand.

"I had to wait for you to come back so I could give you your gift," Blair smiled, far too wide to be genuine.

It was an isolated night. No one was around. Not a single voice or sound in sight. It was dark, and Blair could not see the vicinity beyond her five-hundred-foot radius. It was the perfect spot, the perfect time.

"Oh, what is it?" Aiden asked.

"It's on the hood of my car. Go see for yourself!"

As Aiden walked over to Blair's car and unwrapped the present, Blair crept up behind him, pulled a knife from her pocket, and stood close behind Aiden.

She breathed into his ear, nibbling on it and whispering, "You were always my most tragic love."

Before Aiden had the chance to speak, he felt a small knife jab through his side. He turned around and faced Blair, who continuously stabbed him over and over with the pocket knife, refusing to stop until she was sure Aiden had lost enough blood to die.

"I hate you! I hate you! I hate you!" Blair echoed as she stabbed Aiden's weakened and mangled body.

"I love you so much!! I love you, Aiden. I love you. It's your fault I have to do this!"

Blair's anger and fury had quickly turned to sadness and sorrow. She held Aiden's corpse close to her, and she continued to cry.

"I'm sorry, my love."

She kissed Aiden on the forehead before jabbing her knife through it.

Terrified of what she had just done, she picked up Aiden's body and threw it into her trunk. She was too fatigued and dejected to figure out a better solution to dump his body.

"I'll just figure it out in the morning."

***

To Blair's eventual demise, she had been so busy trying to get the image of Aiden and Alex out of her mind that she had completely forgotten about the corpse of Aiden in her trunk.

Over the next few days, she was preoccupied with hooking up with random men she met on a dating app called "Slutter" that she failed to remember what she had done.

One week after the incident, Blair was fooling around in bed with a blonde-hair man named Elijah, who was twice her age, when the news about Aiden's death came on. However, Blair was too busy pleasuring Elijah that she failed to realize what was on the news.

"It has been nearly a week since the disappearance of 30-year-old Aiden Mzithial. According to a familial source, he was last seen driving toward Lake Kwala with his boat and has not been heard from since. His partner, Alex Flinch, reported seeing him walk back toward his car, a light blue Mercedes, license place ILY-7934, after she had parted with him the night of his disappearance. However, she reported that it was too dark for her to see whether anyone else was with him. If anyone has information about the location of this man, please contact 9-1-1 immediately."

"I love you," Blair whispered to Elijah after they were finished having sex.

"Wait, hold up. Love? Nah, nah man. That ain't cool. We just met. There's no love. Please leave. I don't think we should see each other again," Elijah fearfully said as he pushed Blair out the door.

Distraught and still heavily drunk, Blair got into her car and began driving home, only stopping once to prostitute herself and buy a bottle of rum before passing out on her bed.

***

The next morning, Blair heard a loud scream.

"Blair!" Her mother screamed up at her from downstairs.

"Wha...?" Blair mumbled.

She cannot remember what had happened last night. All she could remember was drinking too much and getting kicked out of Club Baron for vomiting on the DJ. She couldn't even remember how she got home.

"Blair! Get your ass down here right now!" Her father screamed.

After a few more minutes of no response from Blair, her mother screamed up one more time.

"Blair, honey! Please come down here. There are some policemen who want to speak with you."

'Police? What? Why?' Blair thought. She had completely forgotten about the night she stabbed Aiden with her overwhelming anger.

She rummaged through her closet and changed into something more revealing, hoping to snag the numbers of the cops, quickly brushed her hair, and gracefully waltzed downstairs where she saw two policemen standing by the door.

"What's going on?" Blair asked innocently.

"Are you Blair Pevensie?" One of the cops asked.

"Yeah, why?"

"Were you in contact with a man named Aiden Mzithial last week?"

"Um...I think? I can't remember. Why, what's up? Is everything okay?"

"We received an anonymous call that Aiden Mzithial was last seen with you before his disappearance."

"Disappearance? What?" Blair asked, still displaying innocence.

Blair remembered going out to see Aiden, but she had trouble recalling what had happened that night.

"Ma'am, we're going to need you to open your trunk."

"Blair, honey! What's going on? What's happening?" Mrs. Pevensie anxiously asked.

"I didn't do anything wrong. You don't need to search me. I don't know what you're talking about!" Blair tried to defend herself.

"Miss, please open your trunk now!"

Fearful and still confused at the situation, Blair grabbed her keys, slowly walked over to her car, and popped her trunk.

To everyone's disbelief, including Blair's, Aiden's rotting corpse was found in the trunk, covered in dried blood.

"What?" Blair asked. "I swear I don't know how this happened! I would never do this! I loved him! I didn't do this! I was framed!

Blair continued to scream as the cops tackled her to the ground, refusing to listen to another word. Tears flowed from her eyes as she could not believe that the love of her life, Aiden, was dead.

She tried hard to remember that night, not for the sake of the cops, but because she needed to know if there was truly something wrong with her. How could she not remember something as heinous as murder?

"Blair Pevensie, you are under arrest for the murder of Aiden Mzithial. You have the right to remain silent. Anything you say can be used against you in a court of law. You have the right to a lawyer during further questioning. If you cannot afford a lawyer, one will be appointed to you."

"Blair!" Blair heard her mother cry out as she tried to struggle away from handcuffs on the ground, just before everything went dark.

***

"After serious consideration from the jury, the court has come to a conclusion that Blair Pevensie is guilty, guilty of first-degree murder of Aiden Mzithial, guilty of first-degree assault, guilty of first-degree abduction, and guilty of first-degree police evasion. The court hereby sentences you to 25 years in Schannes Correctional Facility.

However, due to further psych evaluation, the court has decided that your mental health has allowed you to plead guilty on accounts of mental insanity, thereby reducing your sentence to one year in Schannes Correctional Facility and 10 years in Eloquoia Psychiatric Facility, release date to be determined. Court dismissed."

PSYCHOSIA
THE UNEXPLAINED DISORDER

CHAPTER SEVEN

Forgotten

"She's not getting out of here, is she?" Kiersten asks Gwenneth.

"I'll be honest with you, Kiers. Blair suffers from a mental disease known as 'Psychosia'. Psychosia is a very rare mental illness, so rare that there isn't a list of standard criteria to categorize and define it. This disease mainly affects young adults who have dealt with traumatic childhood experiences, causing them to engage in romantic and antagonistic relationships with forces that do not exist.

Over the past year, we have carefully monitor Blair and her nonexistent romantic relationship with someone named Aiden. Aiden was a man that Blair fabricated as a source of comfort from her abusive family. However, as time went on, Blair was no longer able to distinguish the difference between fantasy and reality, manifesting her inner conflict with herself in her imaginary relationship with Aiden.

This illness causes people to behave and act out in erratic ways that they usually do not remember the next day. It causes people to engage in behaviors outside their moral conscience, acting out based on their feelings rather than their logic. They engage in actions that they seem to have no conscience or guilt toward until years down the line, and they bounce back and forth from being innocent and sweet to dangerous and deadly.

I'm afraid Blair is stuck here for life. We cannot, in good conscience, release her back into the public with her mindset. It would be fatal to everyone she encounters. We will keep her here. We will not send her to death row where she likely belongs, but I'm afraid she will never see the light of day ever again."

"Can she still have visitors? Can her family still visit her?" Kiersten asks.

"It doesn't seem likely that they ever will again given what happened the last time they were here, but I'm sorry, she will remain estranged from everyone. She can no longer wander throughout the walls of the hospital; she can only remain in her room. No one in, no one out.

You will no longer be able to enter Blair's room like you used to. Blair will remain locked inside, receiving her meals and her meds through a small slit on the door," Gwenneth continues.

"Is there anything we can do to help her? Can she ever heal from this?"

"We've tried every medicine we could think of. She refuses to take most of them, and she has not been complying with her therapy sessions. We're all doing the best we can, but there is only so much we can do when the patient refuses to accept help.

Psychosic patients are rarely open to treatment because they refuse to believe there is something wrong with them to begin with that require treatment. I believe

Blair is a lost cause. She will simply ride out her days here until she dies. I'm sorry," Gwenneth says her final words and walks away.

Feeling defeated, Kiersten walks by Blair's room, opens the slit, and sees her rocking back and forth in her red gown. She has never seen her this bad before. Blair's memories are really taking a toll on her as all she has done lately is sit in her room, pulling strands of her hair out.

Blair cannot stop thinking about the night she murdered Aiden. Every time she tries to fall asleep, she pictures the limp and rotting body of Aiden in the trunk of her car, the moment that took away her sanity and freedom forever.

She is finally starting to accept that she is a murderer. However, rather than accepting treatment for her condition, Blair becomes extremely suicidal, hating herself and unable to snap herself out of her depressive thoughts.

She reflects on one of the last fights she had with Aiden before they broke up, a senseless fight over a stupid bottle of alcohol.

***

Aiden stumbled home one night way past midnight, drunk as an alcoholic while carrying a bottle of vodka, and puked on their $400 rug. He had been out all night with his friends without a single call or text to let Blair know where he was or when he was coming home. He reeked of alcohol, and their beautiful rug was ruined.

"Yo," Aiden said after he picked himself up from vomiting, only to drop his head back down to puke some more.

Blair had become tired of Aiden pulling stunts like this on her. Just last month, he had spent their entire savings on casinos and hookers, failing to let Blair know what had happened until she discovered a negative balance in their bank account a week later. She was tired of Aiden acting irresponsibly and spending all her money because he never bothered to get a job.

"I said...yo," Aiden repeated himself as he chugged a quarter bottle of his vodka and burped obnoxiously.

Blair refused to acknowledge him. Nothing she wanted to say to him would lead to anything positive, and anything she could say to him were lies. Besides, nothing she said ever registered through his thick head; he just hears what he wanted to hear.

Plopping himself next to her, still reeking the stench of booze and his bottle in one hand, he leaned over toward Blair and pressured her for a kiss.

"Come on. Give me some sugar, love."

"No, Aiden. You're drunk. You need to get yourself and my rug cleaned up. You're disgusting."

"Come on, just one kiss."

Aiden then moved his hand up Blair's thigh and attempted to unbutton her jeans. He slobbered over her as he licked her neck and continued to pressure her for sex.

"Back off, Aiden! I don't want to!"

"But I want to. And I know part of you want to also. Come here, my love," Aiden kept repeating as he pounced on top of Blair.

"I said, fuck off!"

Blair pushed so hard that Aiden fell onto the ground, cracking his tooth on the coffee table in the process.

"What the fuck, bitch! What the fuck is wrong with you?" Aiden shouted as blood dripped down his bottom lip.

However, he was too numb from the alcohol to feel the pain.

"What the fuck is wrong with me?! What the fuck is wrong with you?"

"What are you talking about!? You're the one who pushed me!"

"Me? You can't just walk in here in the middle of the night, drunk, vomit on my rug, and then try to feel me up!"

"You're my girlfriend. If I want to feel you up, I'll feel you up. You're my property. You're mine!"

"Fuck you! I don't belong to you! You can't just do things to me whenever you feel like it!"

This time Aiden became angrier. He pinned Blair down and began tearing off her shirt with his teeth, biting into her skin.

"Get off me! Get off me!" Blair screamed as she tried to push Aiden off her.

However, Aiden continued trying to rape her as Blair struggled to get away. She then spotted Aiden's bottle of vodka, pulled herself toward it, grabbed it, and knocked the bottle across Aiden's head, causing him to pass out as blood gushed from his cranium.

***

Blair spent the next three months in solitary confinement, unable to leave the small quarters of her cell. Her therapy sessions had been discontinued because the doctors no longer saw them as helpful.

Blair was not responding to anything they tried, so the hospital figured the best treatment is to keep her in isolation, away from those who still have a fighting chance.

Day Seven Progress Update

Blair has been lying on the ground in her cell for the past several days. She shows no signs of movement, only heavy and spontaneous breathing. Her wounds are beginning to heal just as fresh ones are being created.

No one has gone into her chamber since she has been ordered into confinement. No one is daring enough to enter her parameters. Will she ever get up? Or will she die in that very same spot?

Day Twenty Progress Update

Blair has finally gotten up but has been frozen in one corner of her cell indefinitely. She just sits and rocks back and forth, chanting, "I'm not worthy. I'm not worthy." When one of the nurses knocked on her door, Blair hissed and shrieked at her to go away. She refuses to eat. The food that she is given are being thrown against the wall.

Day Thirty-Five Progress Update

Blair has been spotted writing on the walls with her own blood. A few of the words include, "Slut," "Bitch," "Liar," "Psycho," and "Die." She bites into her arms to generate more blood, which she uses to continue writing. Day and night, she does this, only stopping when she feels lightheaded from the loss of oxygen.

Day Fifty Progress Update

Blair is seen speaking to herself again. She throws herself across her cell, screaming at herself to go away. She seems to be having a personal mental battle with her own body. She seems to be arguing with an invisible force that does not answer back.

Day Eighty Progress Update

Blair's meals have been taken away from her as she refuses to eat and simply throws them against the wall, letting them rot. She has now gone almost three months without food and is wasting away. How she is still alive, is a mystery. She must be eating her own flesh or excrements to stay alive.

The doctors and nurses no longer know how to handle her. We will check on her in a few days, but we are simply waiting it out until she finally starves to death or commits suicide.

"I can't live like this anymore. I have destroyed the lives of everyone around me. There is no recovering from what I did. I will never get to leave. What's the point of even living anymore? There is no hope for me in this world."

Blair lifts her mattress and tries to yank out one of the bronze wires. However, it refuses to budge so she gnaws on it with her teeth. She is determined to get this wire off the bed. She continues gnawing, breaking several teeth, until she finally pulls one loose.

Staring at her left wrist, she punctures herself, slicing all the veins inside her wrist and bleeding until she is covered in more blood than her body contains. It is finally her time to die. She needs to relieve herself from this world. As she lies still in her blood, she begins to sing.

"You are the only one I'll ever love.
You are the only one I'll ever need.
Come back and save me.
Save me from myself.
You took my heart and shattered it to dust.
You took my spirit and stabbed it until it bled.
You took my innocence and turned me into a killer.
I am left with nothing.
I am nothingness.
I do not deserve love.
I do not deserve to be known.
I do not deserve life.
Perish me."

"I'm sorry, Blair," Blair whispers one last time.

And with her last breath, she sees her life flash before her eyes as she falls into her own pool of blood, alone and isolated from the world, just like how she lived.

Day Ninety-Eight Progress Update
Blair is found dead in her forgotten prison.
***

The next morning, Kiersten enters Blair's cell after her body had been taken out to the courtyard to be burned. Eloquoia has more body counts than any other hospital facility in the nation, and with zero funding and cramped morgue spaces, they are forced to burn the bodies of the dead.

Still devastated by the death of her favorite patient, Kiersten looks around Blair's cell to say her final condolences. However, as she exits, she notices that the ground is covered in words, words written in blood. During Blair's final hour, she had written letters to her parents, Aiden, and Kiersten with her final words of farewell.

"Dear Mom and Dad,

You were always my role models. I looked up to you growing up, but all you seemed to ever do was hit me and each other. You always wondered why I rebelled, why I refused to listen to your orders, why I had become so disobedient and promiscuous.
It was because of you guys. I wanted love from you, but all I ever received were either a fist or useless trinkets I didn't even want. I had to look for love and comfort elsewhere because I feared going to you.
Somewhere down the line, I thought acting out would make you pay attention to me, would make you love me, but instead, you just blamed me for every flaw I ever had. Once, just once, I wish you had accepted me for who I was."

"Dear Aiden,
I have a confession. I don't love you. I never loved you. I was addicted to you. You showed interest in me when no one else did and when I was beginning to lose hope of ever finding love.
Before I met you, I tried finding love in others by having sex with them. I did the same with you, but you were different. You stayed. Now I wish you hadn't. I remember now. I remember killing you.
But you deserved it. You abused me and cheated on me right before my very eyes. What else was I supposed to do? I trusted you! I think I will always see you as the man who ruined my life. I hope you scorch in hell."

"Dear Kiersten,
Of all the people I have ever met, you were the only one who ever truly believed in me. You treated me like I was your own, and you cared for me.
There were many moments where I felt hopeful for recovery because I thought you believed in me.

So, I tried. For you! But I couldn't stop thinking that you were only doing so because it was your job, not because you really cared. I need to know.
Did you truly care about me, or did you just want the pay raise for dealing with the toughest patient in this hospital?"

"Clean up this mess," Kiersten orders the custodian as she walks out the gated door and slams it behind her.

PSYCHOSIA
THE UNEXPLAINED DISORDER

PSYCHOSIA
THE UNEXPLAINED DISORDER

PSYCHOSIA
THE UNEXPLAINED DISORDER

Your mind is your greatest enemy

PSYCHOSIA
THE UNEXPLAINED DISORDER

PSYCHOSIA
THE UNEXPLAINED DISORDER

PSYCHOSIA
THE UNEXPLAINED DISORDER